D0646983

WEST SLOPE COMMUNITY LIBRARY
(503) 292-6416
MEMBER OF
WASHINGTON COUNTY COOPERATIVE
LIBRARY SERVICES

Biscuit's Christmas
Storybook Collection

by Alyssa Satin Capucilli   pictures by Pat Schories

HARPER
An Imprint of HarperCollinsPublishers

Table of Contents

HarperFestival is an imprint of HarperCollins Publishers.

Biscuit's Christmas Storybook Collection
Text copyright © 2013 by Alyssa Satin Capucilli
Illustrations copyright © 2013 by Pat Schories

Biscuit's Christmas
Text copyright © 2000 by Alyssa Satin Capucilli
Illustrations copyright © 2000 by Pat Schories

Biscuit's Show and Share Day
Text copyright © 2007 by Alyssa Satin Capucilli
Illustrations copyright © 2007 by Pat Schories

Biscuit's Christmas Eve
Text copyright © 2007 by Alyssa Satin Capucilli
Interior illustrations copyright © 2007 by HarperCollins Publishers

Biscuit Wants to Play
Text copyright © 2001 by Alyssa Satin Capucilli
Interior illustrations copyright © 2001 by Pat Schories

Biscuit Gives a Gift
Text copyright © 2004 by Alyssa Satin Capucilli
Interior illustrations copyright © 2004 by Pat Schories

Biscuit Visits the Big City
Text copyright © 2006 by Alyssa Satin Capucilli
Interior illustrations copyright © 2006 by Pat Schories

Biscuit's Snowy Day
Text copyright © 2005 by Alyssa Satin Capucilli
Interior illustrations copyright © 2005 by Pat Schories

Biscuit and the Lost Teddy Bear
Text copyright © 2011 by Alyssa Satin Capucilli
Interior illustrations copyright © 2011 by Pat Schories

Biscuit Goes to School
Text copyright © 2002 by Alyssa Satin Capucilli
Interior illustrations copyright © 2002 by Pat Schories

All rights reserved.
Manufactured in China.
No part of this book may be used or reproduced in any manner whatsoever without
written permission except in the case of brief quotations embodied in critical articles
and reviews. For information address HarperCollins Children's Books, a division of
HarperCollins Publishers, 10 East 53rd Street, New York, NY 10022.
www.harpercollinschildrens.com
ISBN 978-0-06-228842-4
Book design by Leslie Mechanic and Victor Ochoa
13 14 15 16 17   SCP   10 9 8 7 6 5 4 3 2 1

First Edition

Biscuit's Christmas

"Come along, Biscuit," called the little girl.
"Christmas is almost here.
It's time to choose our tree."
Woof, woof!

"This tree is just the right size, Biscuit."
Woof, woof!
"Oh, Biscuit! You found a pinecone!"

"Mmm-mm! I smell hot chocolate!"
Woof, woof!

"Silly puppy!
How did you get those marshmallows?"

"We have everything we need
to trim the tree, Biscuit.
We have our friends, our family,
and lots of decorations."

Woof, woof!

"No, no, Biscuit!"

Bow wow!

"No tugging, Puddles!
The popcorn is for the tree!"

"It's time to put the star at the very top!"

Woof, woof!
"Wait, Biscuit!"
Come back with that candy cane!"

"The stockings are hung.
Let's have some apple cider
and sing Christmas carols!"

Woof, woof!

"Biscuit, what are you doing?"

Woof, woof!
"Funny puppy, you are right!

I almost forgot to leave gingerbread and milk
for Santa Claus!"

"Oh, Biscuit, don't you just love the
sweet smell of Christmas?"

Biscuit's
Show and Share Day

"Today is show and share day at school, Biscuit.
What shall I bring to show and share with my class?"
Woof, woof!

"Maybe I will bring my favorite teddy bear."
Woof, woof!

"Funny puppy!
You found your favorite blanket."
Woof!

"A seashell would be fun to show and share,
or a picture of the new baby!"
Woof, woof!

"Silly puppy!
It's not time to play ball now.
It's almost time for school."

27

"Now, let's see. What shall I bring?"
Woof, woof! Woof, woof!
"Oh, no, Biscuit.
How did you get that box of biscuits?"
Woof!

Beep! Beep!
"There's the school bus, Biscuit.
It's time for school!"
Woof, woof!

"Wait, Biscuit. Come back!
Where are you going with my backpack?"
Woof, woof!

"Oh, Biscuit.
You want to go to school today.
You want to be my show and share!"
Woof, woof!

"I can hardly wait for everyone to meet you, Biscuit.
Come along, sweet puppy!
There's my teacher."
Woof, woof!

"Welcome to school, Biscuit.
This is going to be the most special
show and share day of all!"
Woof, woof!

Biscuit's Christmas Eve

"It's Christmas Eve, Biscuit."
Woof, woof!

"It's the night before Christmas, and we have lots to do."
Woof!

"Our Christmas tree is trimmed
with beautiful decorations.
Which one is your favorite, Biscuit?"

Woof, woof!
"Funny puppy!
That decoration looks just
like your ball!"
Woof!

"It's time to hang the Christmas stockings, Biscuit.
Soon Santa Claus will fill them with wonderful treats!"

"This one says, Biscuit!"
Woof, woof!
"Silly puppy!
Come back with that stocking!"
Woof!

"It's fun to make a Christmas gift for friends and family, Biscuit.
Mom and Dad will love this painting of us!
Now, where can the wrapping paper be?"

Woof, woof!
"Oh, Biscuit.
You found the
wrapping paper . . .

. . . and the ribbon!"
Woof!

"Listen, Biscuit!
Do you hear
what I hear?"

Woof, woof!
Woof, woof!

"It's the
Christmas carolers!
Let's sing along!
Fa la la la la!"
Woof!

"It just wouldn't be Christmas without cookies
and milk for Santa Claus and his reindeer, Biscuit."
Woof, woof!

"M-m-m.
They smell delicious!"
Woof!
"Don't worry, Biscuit!
There's a treat for you, too!"
Woof!

51

"We're all ready, Biscuit.
I can hardly wait
for Christmas!"
Woof, woof!

"Curl up, Biscuit.
Let's share a Christmas
story while we wait
for Santa Claus!"
Woof!

Z-z-z-z-z!
Z-z-z-z-z!

"Hooray! Wake up, sleepy puppy!
Christmas is here at last!"
Woof, woof! Woof, woof!

"Oh, Biscuit. The very best part of Christmas
is sharing it with a sweet puppy like you!"
Woof, woof!

"Merry Christmas, Biscuit!"

Biscuit
Wants to Play

Woof, woof!

What's in the basket,

Biscuit?

Meow.

It's Daisy!

Meow. Meow.

Daisy has two kittens.

Woof, woof!
Biscuit wants to play
with the kittens.

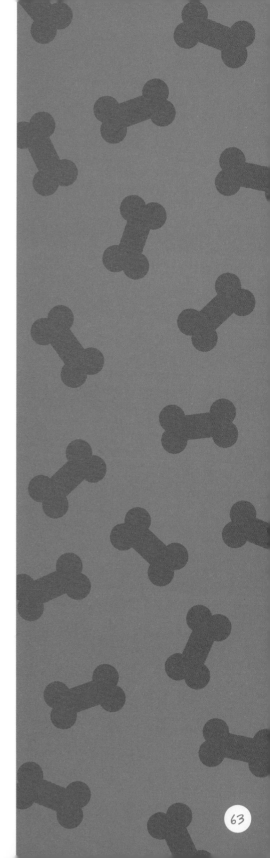

Meow. Meow.

The kittens want to play

with a leaf.

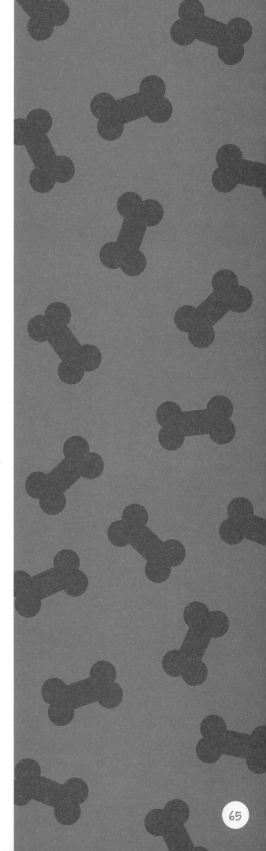

Woof, woof!

Biscuit wants to play too.

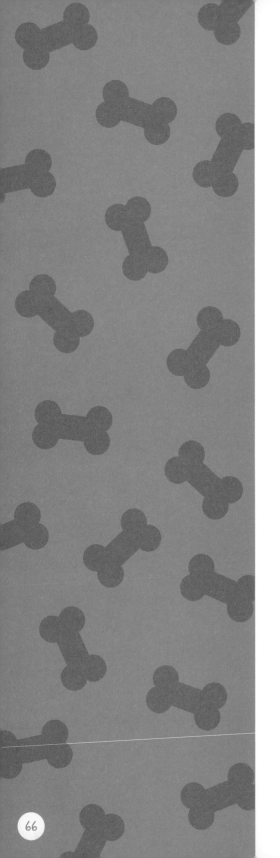

Woof!

Biscuit sees his ball.

Meow. Meow.

The kittens see a cricket.

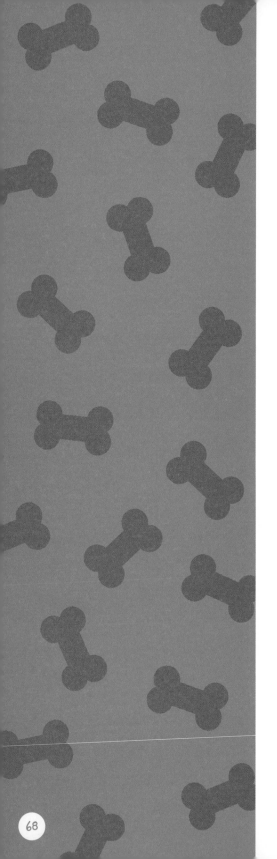

Woof, woof!

Biscuit wants to play, too!

Meow. Meow.

The kittens see a butterfly.

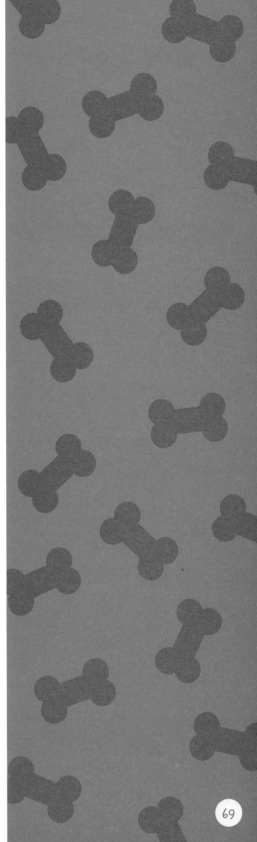

69

Meow. Meow.

The kittens run.

The kittens jump.

Meow! Meow!
The kittens are stuck
in the tree!

72

Woof!
Biscuit sees
the kittens.

Woof, woof, woof!

Biscuit can help the kittens!

Woof, woof!

Biscuit wants to play
with the kittens.

Meow! Meow!

The kittens want to play

with Biscuit, too!

Biscuit Gives a Gift

"Wake up, sleepy puppy!
It's Christmas, and we have
lots to do."

Woof, woof!

"We're going to give some special gifts
to our neighbors, friends, and family, Biscuit."
Woof, woof!

"Oh, Biscuit! Wait for me."
Woof!

"These mittens are so warm and cozy.
We can hang them on the mitten tree."

Woof, woof!

"Silly puppy!
No tugging, Biscuit."

"This way, Biscuit.
Grandma and Grandpa will love
the gingerbread we baked."
Woof, woof!

"Funny puppy!
No cookies for you!"
Woof!

"Sharing a story is one of the
best gifts of all."
Woof, woof!

"Curl up, Biscuit. You can
hear the story, too."
Woof!

"Gifts come in all shapes
and sizes, Biscuit.
We can give birdseed to the birds."

"And big crunchy biscuits to friends like Puddles and Sam."

Woof, woof!

"Sweet puppy!
A kiss from you is the best
Christmas gift ever!"
Woof!

Biscuit Visits the Big City

Here we are, Biscuit.

Woof, woof!

We're in the big city.

We're going to visit

our friend Jack.

Woof, woof!

Coo, coo!

Stay with me, Biscuit.

It's very busy in the big city!

Woof, woof!

There are lots of tall buildings
in the big city, Biscuit.
Woof, woof!

107

There are lots of people, too.

Woof, woof!

Funny puppy!
You want to say hello
to everyone.

109

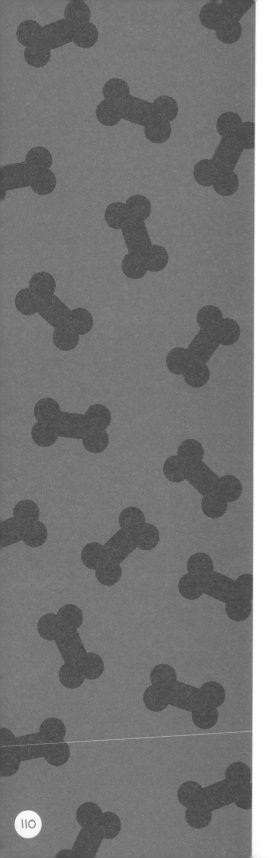

Stay with me Biscuit.

It's very busy here!

Woof, woof!

Beep! Beep!

Woof!

It's only a big bus, Biscuit.

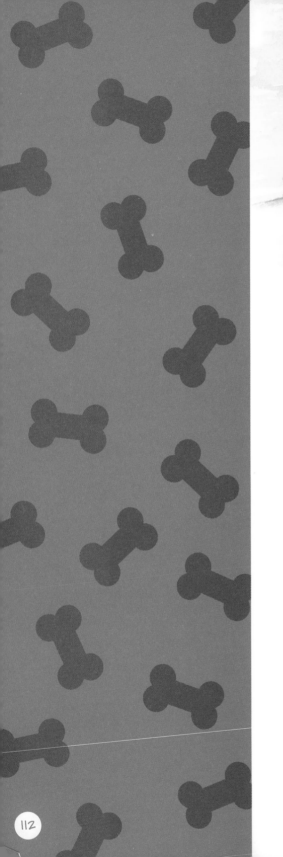

Woof, woof!

You found the fountain,

Biscuit.

There's so much to see
in the big city,
isn't there, Biscuit?

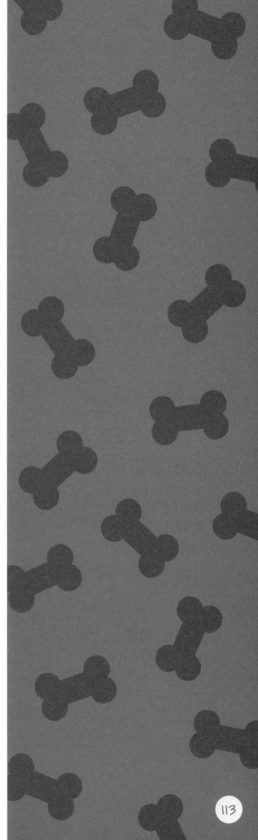

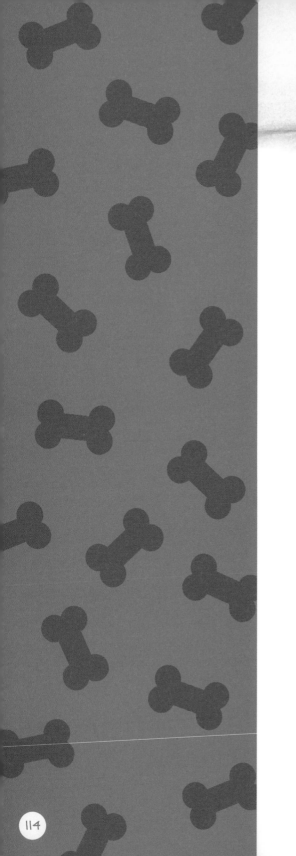

Woof!

Coo, coo!

Woof, woof!

Coo, coo!

Woof, woof! Woof, woof!

Oh no, Biscuit! Come back!

Biscuit, where are you going?

Woof!

Silly puppy! Here you are.

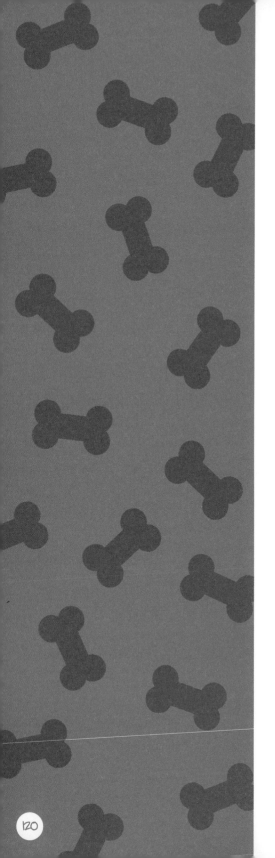

This is a big, busy city, Biscuit.

But you found our friend Jack,

and some new friends, too!

Coo, coo!

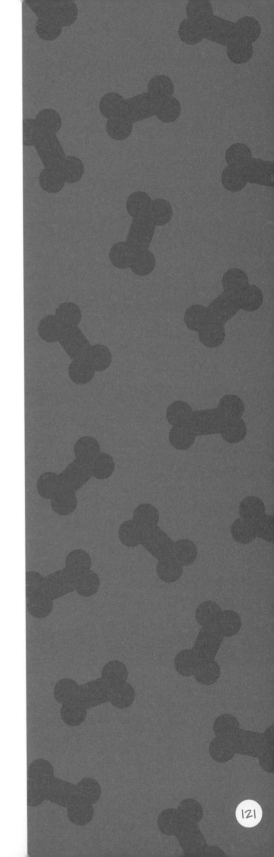

Woof!

Biscuit's Snowy Day

"Come along, Biscuit. It's snowing!
We're going to have a great snowy day!"
Woof, woof!

"I'll put on my mittens and boots."
Woof, woof!

"And here's a cozy sweater for you.
Let's go, sweet puppy!"
Woof!

"We're all going to build a snowman, Biscuit.
Everyone can help roll a big, big snowball!"
Woof, woof!

"Funny puppy!
That's the way!"
Woof!

"Oh, Biscuit!
You found the snowman's scarf and hat!"
Woof, woof!

"You found his carrot nose, too!
What do you think, Biscuit?"
Woof!

"The snow is so soft and powdery.
It's perfect for making snow angels."

"And snow puppies, too."
Woof, woof!
Bow, wow!

"Look, Biscuit. It's time to go sledding!
Hold on tight, sweet puppy."
Woof, woof!

"Here we go!"
Woof!

"There's nothing like a great snowy day, Biscuit.
There's hot cocoa and treats."
Woof, woof!

"And lots of fun for all!"

Biscuit and the Lost Teddy Bear

Woof, woof!

What do you see, Biscuit?

Is it a bird?

Woof, woof!

Is it a butterfly?

Woof, woof!

Oh, Biscuit.

It is a teddy bear!

Woof, woof!

Somebody lost a teddy bear.

Who can it be?

Woof, woof!

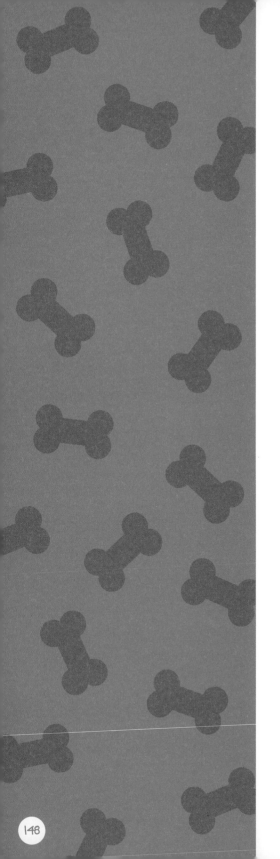

Woof, woof!

Is this your teddy bear, Sam?

Ruff!

No. It is not Sam's bear.

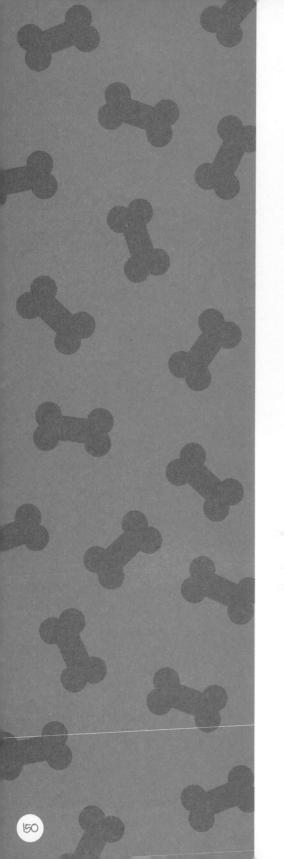

Woof, woof!

Is this your teddy bear, Puddles?

Bow wow!

No. It is not Puddles's bear.

Woof, woof!

Someone lost a teddy bear.

But who can it be?

Woof, woof!

Wait, Biscuit.

What do you see now?

153

Woof!

Biscuit sees a big truck.

Woof!

Biscuit sees a lot of boxes.

Woof, woof!

Biscuit sees a little boy, too.

Woof, woof! Woof, woof!

Is this your teddy bear,

little boy?

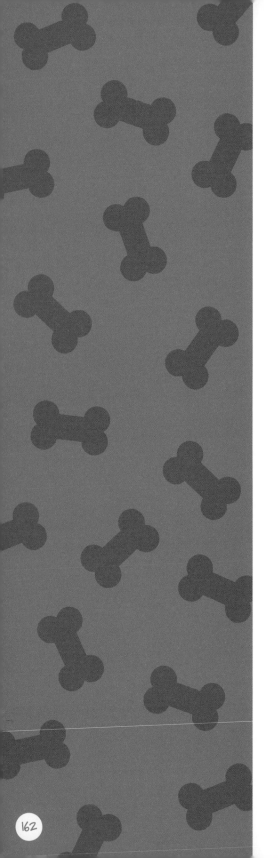

Yes. It is!

Woof!

The little boy
lost his teddy bear, Biscuit,
but you found it!
Woof, woof!

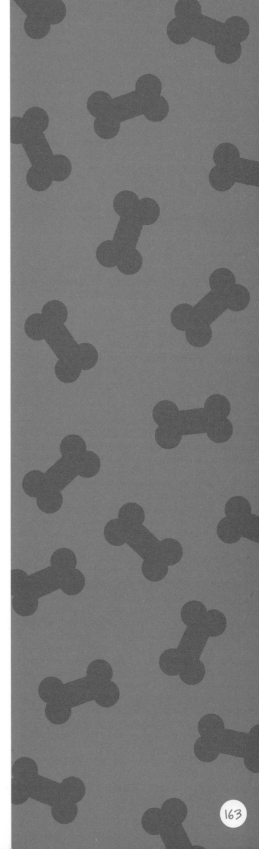

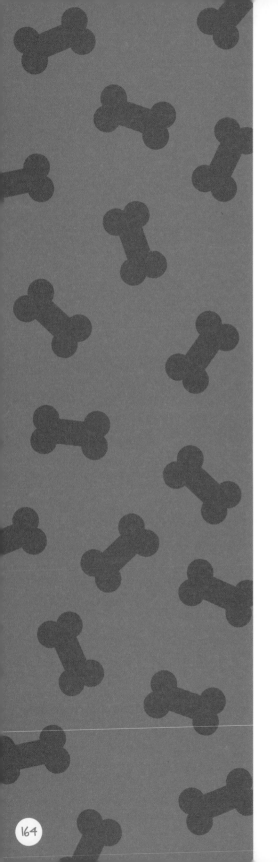

The teddy bear gets a big hug.

Woof, woof!

And Biscuit gets a big hug, too!

Woof!

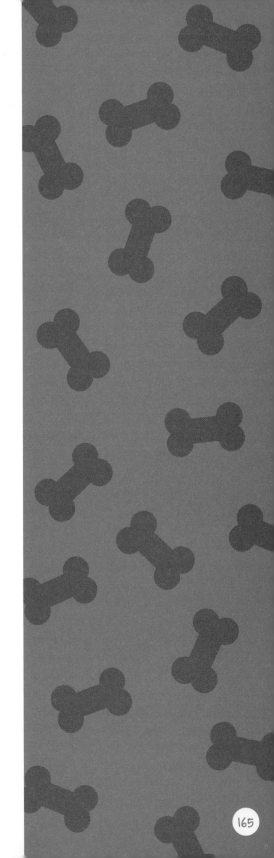

Biscuit
Goes to School

Here comes the school bus!

Woof, woof!

Stay here, Biscuit.

Dogs don't go to school.

Woof!

Where is Biscuit going?

Is Biscuit going to the pond?

Woof!

Is Biscuit going to the park?

Woof!

Biscuit is going to school!

Woof, woof!

Biscuit wants to play ball.

Woof, woof!

Biscuit wants
to hear a story.
Woof, woof!
Shhh!

179

Biscuit wants a snack.

Woof, woof!

Oh, Biscuit!

What are you doing here?

Dogs don't go to school!

Oh, no!

Here comes the teacher!

Woof!

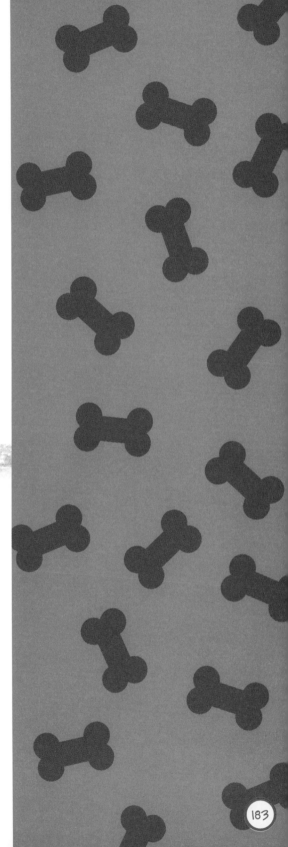

Biscuit wants

to meet the teacher.

Woof!

Biscuit wants

to meet the class.

Woof, woof!

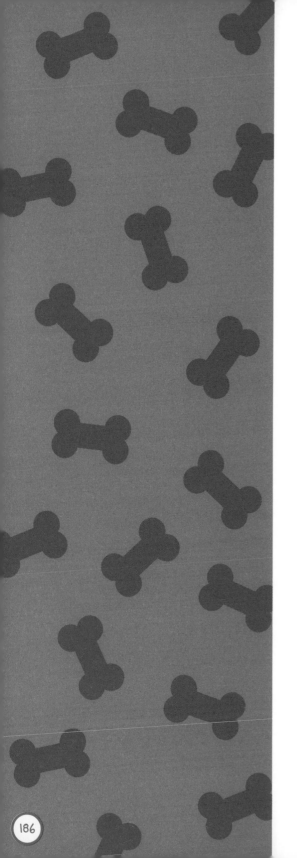

Biscuit likes school!

Woof, woof!

And everyone at school

likes Biscuit!

Woof!

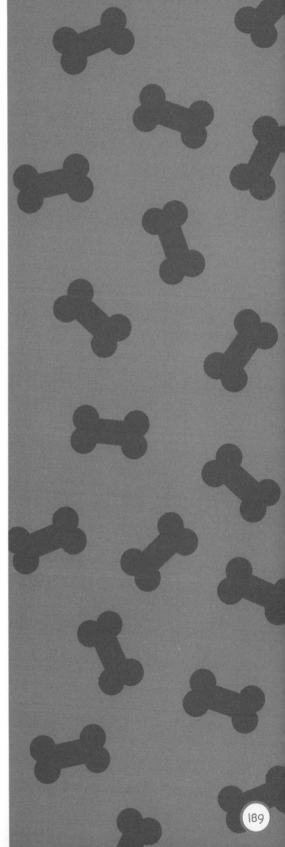

The End

12/14 E
CAP